VICTORY FOR JAMIE

WALTER DEAN MYERS

Illustrations by Norm Walker

Copyright © 1989, 1977 by Walter Dean Myers.
All rights reserved. Published by Scholastic Inc.
SPRINT and SPRINT BOOKS are trademarks of Scholastic Inc.
Printed in the U.S.A.
ISBN 0-590-35207-5

7 8 9 10   31   03 02 01 00 99 98

CHAPTER 1

Jamie Davis took his last foul shots. He had done fairly well in the tryouts. But he still wasn't sure that he was going to make the team. Four more boys still had to take their shots. Jamie watched them. Mr. Reese was the coach of the basketball team. He had said that there were only four more spots left. Jamie wondered if he was going to fill one of them.

Jamie was in the sixth grade at Madison. He had never tried out for a team before. But Jamie played basketball after school all the time. He knew he was good, but was he good enough to make the team? Usually it took all his efforts just to keep his grades up. His problem was that he was nearly deaf. Even with his hearing aid he could hear only loud noises. So Jamie had to learn to lip-read.

Jamie hadn't thought about trying out for the team. It was his best friend Peter who said that he should. He decided that he would.

The tryouts had three parts. First they had to dribble around the gym as fast as they could. Mr. Reese timed each player. Jamie didn't do too well on the dribbling. But neither did the other boys. For the second part of the tryouts they played a three-man game. Jamie played with Mark White

and a boy named Billy. His team didn't do well at all. The first team to make ten points was the winner. The other team had six points before Jamie's team scored their first. The best player on the other team was guarding Jamie. Jamie had a chance to shoot once. But the ball hit the rim and bounced away. His team lost ten to six. Jamie had four rebounds but no baskets.

The last part of the tryouts was shooting foul shots. Each boy had to shoot five times. Most of the boys made two or three shots. Jamie made only

one. He didn't think he was going to make the team.

After the last boy had shot, Mr. Reese called some of the boys over. He talked to them and then they left. Then Mr. Reese went over to the other boys.

"The boys I sent away didn't make the team," he said. "Right now you boys are the team. It is an honor to play for the school. You are all expected to do your best. The first practice is after school tomorrow. Do you all understand?"

Jamie stared at Mr. Reese so he could read his lips. He nodded with the others.

"Also, you must bring a note from home and your doctor saying that you may play. I want every boy to be in the best of health this year. Last year we almost won a championship. This year I hope we can win it."

Jamie was very happy when he got to the locker

room. All the boys were congratulating each other. Some of them didn't know that Jamie was almost deaf. They all shook hands and told him their names. When they learned that he read lips, they talked differently. That made it hard for Jamie to understand them. They didn't know that they should just talk the same. But Jamie was so happy that he didn't mind. He had made the team!

CHAPTER 2

The team worked hard for three weeks before the first practice game. Jamie knew that he was not the best player. But neither was he the worst. He wanted to be a good player and he tried as hard as he could. The school paper had a story about the team. It had the names of all the players. It said how tall they were and what position they played. Jamie was five feet tall and he played forward.

Short Hills was the first practice game Madison was to play. They had to take a bus over to Short Hills. All the players and kids who wanted to see the game rode in one bus. Jamie sat next to Peter. Peter wished him luck. It was an exciting feeling.

When the team came out of the dressing room, Short Hills' team was warming up. Madison warmed up at the other end of the court. After a while a buzzer sounded. Mr. Reese called the team over to the bench.

"All right," he said. "Everyone will get a chance to play. I expect you all to do the best you can. Keep in mind the things we have done in practice." Then he named the starting players. Jamie wasn't going to start but he didn't mind.

The game started and Short Hills got the ball.

They started passing the ball around the outside.
They moved the ball well. Their guard dribbled
across the top of the foul circle. He stopped short
and quickly passed to their center. Their center
turned and put up a lazy hook. It went just over
the fingers of Dean, Madison's center. The ball fell

into the basket without touching the rim. Short
Hills was ahead two to nothing.

Mark and Byran brought the ball down for
Madison. Mark took the first shot. The ball hit the
rim and bounced off. But Dean got the rebound
and put it back up. It went in to tie the game.

Madison was playing well but so was Short Hills. The lead first went to Short Hills, then to Madison, then back again to Short Hills. At half time Madison trailed by four points.

"They're playing a slow game with set plays," Mr. Reese said. "We'll have to make them run faster if we want to win."

The starting five went back in to start the second

half. The Short Hills team seemed very sure of themselves. They moved the ball well and took careful shots. They went ahead by seven points. But then Dean got hot and hit three shots in a row. The team began to move a little faster and soon the score was tied. Jamie was the only man who hadn't gotten into the game. And there were five minutes left to play.

Madison had the ball and a chance to go ahead. Dean passed to Mark who started to dribble but lost the ball. Short Hills got the ball and scored quickly. Then Madison got the ball but Mark was called for walking. When Madison got the ball again Mr. Reese called time out. He told Mark to sit down. Jamie hoped that Mr. Reese would not put him in. He knew that he would make a mistake. Mr. Reese looked at his lineup card. Then he looked at Jamie. He told Jamie to go in.

Madison brought the ball down but did not score. Short Hills now had the ball. Their guard passed it to the man that Dean was guarding. He began to dribble toward Jamie. Jamie watched him carefully. He didn't want to make a mistake. He forgot about his own man for just a minute. Then the man with the ball passed over Jamie's head to his man. Jamie jumped to try to stop the shot but fouled his man. The basket was good and his man made the foul shot.

Madison brought the ball down court. Jamie's hands were sweating. His man was guarding him closely. Byran dribbled past his man near the foul line. He stopped and jumped high into the air. Jamie's man went over to stop Byran's shot. Byran then quickly passed to Jamie. Jamie took a lay-up but it rolled off the rim. He had missed an easy lay-up. Then the buzzer sounded. The game was over and Madison had lost.

Everyone was quiet on the way home. They all felt bad about losing. Mr. Reese didn't say anything. He didn't have to. They knew he was angry at the mistakes they had all made. Mr. Reese and the assistant coach were talking near the front of the bus. Once they turned around and looked toward Jamie. He wondered if they were going to drop him from the team. He was sorry that he had ever tried out.

CHAPTER 3

It was a bad week for Jamie. He couldn't think of anything except basketball. He sat in his classes trying to keep his mind on each subject but he couldn't. He kept thinking about missing that lay-up. He also thought about what Mr. Reese had said the day after they had lost.

"I don't like to lose," he said. "Nobody likes to lose. It's one thing if a team that is better than you beats you. It's another thing if you beat yourselves. There's no excuse for that. If you don't want to play basketball, don't play. If you do, then I expect you to play as well as you can."

All week long they practiced the plays they had not done well. Before the next game Mr. Reese called a meeting. He said not to worry about the last game. But Jamie didn't feel that he really meant it. He said that everyone might not play this time. He wanted his starting five to get more practice. The game was against Dover. It was the last game before the regular season began.

They were playing at Madison and all the kids from school were there. The Madison team had a bad start and Dover took the lead right away. But then Dean and James Turner started making baskets and the score was closer.

Dover had a good team. They were tall too. Once they got the ball down court they scored easily. But they did not have a good ball handler. Mr. Reese called a time-out. He told them to use a full court press. As soon as Dover put the ball inbounds the Madison team was on them.

It was a very close game. At the half Madison had managed to get ahead by two points. The

score was Madison 32, Dover 30.

At half time Mr. Reese talked to the team. He told Dean and Byran to shoot more. He also told Jim Turner that he was playing a very good game. But the starting five were very tired. Jamie knew that they would have to put in some substitutes in the second half. He hoped that Mr. Reese would not put him in.

At the start of the second half Madison played its best basketball. They scored five times in a row. Dover had scored none. Then James Turner had a finger stuck in his eye. It was an accident but it was very painful. James had to leave the game. Then the Madison team seemed to fall apart. Within a few minutes Dover had caught up. The Madison

players were getting tired. Mr. Reese took out Byran and Dean. He put in Mark and another player. They played well. But slowly the Dover team pulled ahead. One player from Dover, number ten, couldn't miss. He hit three short jumpers and went around his man for an easy lay-up.

The Madison students were jumping around and cheering for every play. Jamie could not hear them clearly. But he could see them standing when one of the players scored. On the other side of the gym a crowd of Dover students sat together and cheered when Dover scored.

With only two minutes left to play, Madison had the ball. Mr. Reese called time out. James asked if he could come out. Mr. Reese looked at his bench. Then he motioned to Jamie to go in. Jamie went to the scorer's table and gave his name. Mr. Reese told the team to get the ball down court quickly.

Time was back in and Mark brought the ball down the left side. Dean came out to the foul line and got the pass. Dean started to dribble to his left. He was facing away from the basket. Then he faked a pass to Jamie. Dean turned and went up for the shot. The Dover center hit him across the arm trying to block the shot. The shot missed but Dean made both foul shots. That made the score 37 to 34. Madison was behind by only three points.

Dover took the ball out. They brought it slowly down court. The man with the ball moved across court toward Jamie. This time Jamie watched his own man carefully. The man with the ball stopped and took a shot. The ball hit the back of the rim and bounced off. Dean jumped and tapped the ball to Jamie. Jamie grabbed it and dribbled down court. There was no one between him and the basket. He tried not to think about missing the lay-up. He came down the right side and put the ball softly against the backboard. The ball rested for a moment on the rim and then fell in. He had made it!

He had never felt so good in his life. He turned around to see the other players but the court was empty. Someone had called a time-out. He hadn't heard the referee's whistle. His first basket for Madison didn't count.

CHAPTER 4

Now there was less than a minute left to play. Jamie was surprised that the time went so quickly. Mr. Reese told the team the play he wanted them to use. He wanted either Mark or Byran to take a lay-up.

"That way," he said, "there's a chance that you'll be fouled. Even if you miss we'll still have a chance to score."

When the time-out ended Jamie threw the ball to James Turner. He dribbled the ball to the top of the key and passed to Mark. Mark faked a shot and his man went high into the air. When he jumped Mark went quickly around him for the lay-up. Dover's center switched off and went after Mark. But it was too late. Mark reached the basket and made the lay-up. Now Dover led by only one point. But there were only 30 seconds left to play.

Dover put the ball inbounds and started to stall. They began to pass the ball around the outside. If they were going to shoot they would wait for a good shot. Jamie knew that the game would be over soon if they didn't do something. Jamie gave his man more room. He backed away from him five or six feet. The man with the ball saw Jamie's man clear and passed to him. Jamie knew it would

work. When the ball came to his man he jumped at it. He knocked the ball away but fell down. He looked up and saw that Mark had the ball. Suddenly Mark stopped and looked around. Jamie looked around too.

The referee held his hand up and pointed to Jamie. He had fouled the Dover player. The Dover player went to the foul line. He had two shots and he made both of them. A few seconds later the buzzer sounded. Madison had lost again. And again Jamie had made the last play for his team and failed.

The dressing room was very quiet when Mr. Reese came in. All of the players had their heads down. All except Jamie. Jamie looked at Mr. Reese so that he could see what he was saying.

Mr. Reese said that they had played well. He said that this was a much better game than before. He also said something about Jamie but he couldn't see what he was saying. Mr. Reese had turned away from him as he spoke. At first he thought he might be angry because Jamie had fouled his man. But some of the other players turned toward him and smiled. Whatever Mr. Reese had said it must have been good, Jamie thought.

After they had taken showers, Mr. Reese called Jamie and Mark into his office. He told them that he wanted them to go over to Morristown.

"Morristown has a good team," Mr. Reese said. "Last year they won the Championship. They will probably be the team to beat this year too. If we watch them play maybe we can get an idea on how we should play them. I want you and Mark to watch them carefully and take notes."

The next day after school Mark and Jamie took the bus to Morristown. They got to the gym just before the game began. The Morristown players did not seem very tall. In fact, they were not nearly as tall as the team they would play. But when the game began, Jamie saw how good they really were.

He had never seen a team that could shoot so well. They moved the basketball around well. At the half the Morristown team had a 25-to-12 lead. One of their players, number 12, had scored 20 points all by himself.

"This will be an easy report to make," Mark said. "All we have to say is that they are all great."

Jamie kept his eyes on the Morristown team. They were really good. He wrote down everything he noticed. Mark was right. The Morristown team did look great. He wondered if Madison would stand a chance against them.

On the way home Mark and Jamie compared notes. Jamie had taken down many more things than Mark. They dropped off at the school and went to the gym. The team was still practicing and there was a new boy playing with the team. Jamie watched him practice. He seemed as good as anyone on the team, maybe even better than most. Jamie wondered if anyone was going to be

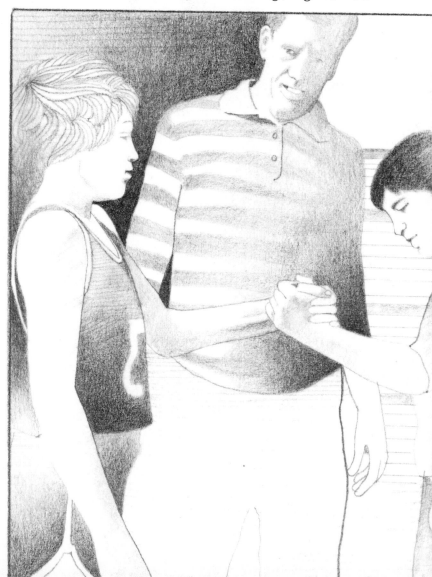

replaced. Mostly he thought about himself.

Mr. Reese took Mark's notes and Jamie's and read them carefully. Then he put them in a file. Later he introduced the new boy to Jamie and Mark.

"This is Joe Kelly. He just moved into Madison and was too late to try out. But if anyone is injured or leaves, Kelly will be our replacement."

CHAPTER 5

It was Madison's first official game of the season. They were going to play Maplewood. Mr. Reese said that he had seen the Maplewood team play. He felt that Madison should beat them. All of the players were excited. They also felt bad for Willie Clark who had to leave the team. In Madison you had to have a B average to play on the team. Willie's average had dropped to a C. Joe Kelly took Willie's place. Willie was surprised that his grades had fallen.

When the game started Maplewood got the ball. They came quickly down court. They passed to their center who turned and shot a hook which went in. Byran threw the ball inbounds for Madison but it was picked off for an easy lay-up. The game was not even a minute long. But the Maplewood squad already had a four-to-nothing lead. Their team was not very tall. But they were always trying to get the ball. Madison seemed to be playing better ball, but by the end of the half the score was very close. Madison had 24 and Maplewood had 22.

During half time Mr. Reese told the team that they were sloppy players. Byran had double dribbled twice. Dean had made three fouls. Jamie had missed two lay-ups. And Mark had the ball taken from him twice.

Mr. Reese seemed to be right in what he said. But it didn't help when they started to play again. Whenever a Madison player got the ball the man guarding him was right on him. Jamie finally scored his first points for Madison. He was fouled once and made the foul shot. Then he made a jumper from the corner.

But still they could not shake the determined Maplewood team. In the last two minutes Maplewood had the lead, 40 to 36. Byran stole the ball and passed it to Mark who scored on the lay-up. But Maplewood was still ahead and they began to slow the ball down. Time was on their side. If neither team scored before the end, Maplewood would win. With a minute and a half to go, Madison put on a full court press.

Maplewood's guard was forced to make a bad pass and it was picked off by Mark. Madison came down fast and Mark passed off to Dean. Dean turned and faked a jump shot. The man guarding him went into the air to block the shot. When he got to the top of his jump Dean went up for his shot. The Maplewood man reached across Dean's arms as he came down. Dean missed the shot but he had been fouled. He would have two chances to make free throws from the line.

Dean went up to the foul line. His first shot went

through the basket without touching the rim. The second shot landed on the rim and rolled around before falling in. Jamie looked over at Dean and saw him breathe a sigh of relief.

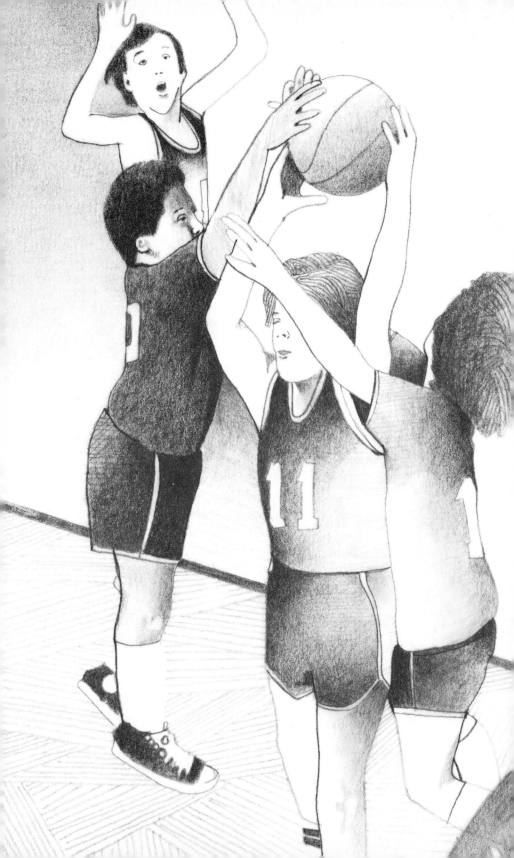

Now the score was tied with only 20 seconds to go. Maplewood had the ball with a chance to score and win the game. This time they were very careful as they brought the ball down. They gave the ball to their best ball handler.

There were only ten seconds left. Then Jamie's man slipped and fell. When he fell Mark motioned for Jamie to go down court. Jamie started running. The Maplewood player became confused. He did

not know his man had fallen. The Maplewood
player shot the ball and missed. Dean grabbed the
rebound and flung it down court. The ball came
right at Jamie. He grabbed it and quickly shot. He
missed the entire backboard. The ball went out of
bounds. A moment later the regular part of the
game was over. Jamie felt bad. If he had made it
Madison would have won. Instead, they had to go
into overtime.

There was a lot of excitement when the overtime period began. Jamie was sitting on the bench. The coach had put Joe Kelly in the game. It was the first time for Kelly.

Madison got the ball and Kelly quickly made two points with a jumper. Dean got the rebound when Maplewood took the next shot. He threw the ball to Kelly on the fast break. Kelly went high into the air for a lay-up. But a Maplewood player went up

with him too. Then Kelly pumped the ball behind his head, twisted and laid it in. The Madison team jumped for joy when they saw him make the basket.

Madison had 12 points in overtime. Kelly had made 10 of the 12 without missing a single shot. He had won the game for Madison. Mr. Reese looked very pleased. He had wanted Madison to win and they had.

CHAPTER 6

Banton, Short Hills, and Grange were the next three games for Madison. They won them all. But the game with Grange was the hardest because Dean had been sick. With Dean out Grange had the height advantage.

James Turner took Dean's place as center. But he wasn't nearly as tall as the Grange center. He was a big kid who wasn't afraid to push. And the referee never seemed to catch him. But things changed in the second half. The referee had called four offensive fouls on the Grange center for pushing. That left him only one more before he had to leave the game. After that he stopped pushing and Madison started pulling in more rebounds. The game was close but Madison won by six points.

The team had been playing well, especially Joe Kelly. But Jamie hardly ever got a chance to play. He didn't play at all against Grange. And he got in the Banton and Short Hills games only when Madison had a big lead.

In practice Jamie would play against Joe Kelly. He was surprised at how well Joe could control his body. He could dribble well with both hands and behind his back. He could dribble quickly and then slow down. It was hard to tell just what he was

going to do. But Jamie liked to play against him. He tried to watch him whenever he played. Soon he found that he could make him miss shots. Sometimes he made him pass the ball away.

During the third week of the schedule Willie Clark showed up at practice. He had a letter from the principal. It said that there had been a mistake in his grade average. He had been given the wrong grade on his history test. His new grade brought his average back up to B. Mr. Reese said that he had been dropped from the team unfairly. Everyone was glad that Willie was back.

They spent the whole practice showing Willie the new plays. Mr. Reese had taken Kelly to the office to talk to him. When practice was over Mr. Reese called the team together and made an announcement.

"As you all know Willie is back with the team. We thought that his grade average had fallen to a C. We were wrong. The school rule is that we make up the team at the beginning of the year. Only if someone is hurt or leaves can someone new get on the team. Now that Willie is back we have to return to our original team. I'm sure that we can win with any team we have."

No one thought much of the speech until after Mr. Reese left and Willie said he was sorry.

"I really want to play," he said. "I wish that Joe could play too."

"Joe? Why isn't he playing?" Byran asked.

"Because he wasn't on the team at the beginning of the year," Willie answered. "That's what Mr. Reese was talking about."

"He's the reason we've been winning," Mark said. "Why don't they just drop the worst player?"

"I guess rules are rules," Willie said.

"And I guess we'll probably start a losing streak."

"I said I'm sorry about Joe," Willie said, slamming his locker shut.

"I'm not talking about you, Willie. Maybe someone else should leave the team."

Jamie felt a lump in his throat. He wanted to say something and he wanted to cry at the same time. He knew they were talking about him. But he wanted to play with the team too. And he had been on the team since the beginning of the year.

Soon word got around that Joe Kelly was not going to play. Jamie saw a few people talking about it. He wondered if they wanted him to leave the team too. He decided not to think about it anymore. And he didn't until he found the note on his desk the next morning.

For Jamie Davis the envelope read. He opened the letter and read the note.

Dear Jamie:

We know that you cannot hear. But we thought that you could see that the only reason the coach keeps you on the team is because you are deaf. Why don't you quit so we can get somebody on the team who can hear and play ball?

Somebody who cares about the team

The tears stung in Jamie's eyes. He could not see the teacher as she spoke. He could not wait for school to be over that day. When it was, he ran all the way home. He went to his room and tried to do his school work. But he couldn't. He still had the

note. He looked at it again and again. He wanted to be part of the team because he could play. Not because he was deaf. He crushed the note and threw it across the room. He had never felt so terrible.

CHAPTER 7

Madison had to win only one more game to play the Championship. The next game was against the Hanover Hawks. The coach had been right. If Madison won the next game they would then play Morristown. Morristown had won all of its games. They would be the team to beat for the Championship.

Hanover was not a very strong team. But Mr. Reese reminded them that they had almost lost to the weak Maplewood team. They could not take any team too lightly. They would have to play their very best.

Hanover had not won many of their games. But the games they had won they won big. And if Madison lost this game they would be out of the Championship.

The Hanover game was the hardest that Madison had ever played. Nothing seemed to go right for them. They missed easy shots and Hanover made hard ones. At half time the score was Hanover 30, Madison 25. Mr. Reese told them that they did not want to win as badly as Hanover did. They weren't trying hard. It was true that the Hanover players were trying as hard as they could. They hustled on every play. They would dive for loose balls. And they tried to block every Madison pass or shot.

"All right, you guys," Mr. Reese said. "The reason you are missing your shots is that you are not taking your time. Don't rush easy shots. When you are double-teamed look for the free man. And don't look so tired out there. Let's move that ball!"

The second half was not much different for
Hanover. They were still making the hard shots.
But now Madison was trying harder too. Dean got
hot and began hitting short jumpers from the line.
Jim Turner began to score and so did Willie Clark.
Slowly but surely the score was tied up.

With a minute to go Dean hit another jump shot and was fouled. Dean made the foul throw and Madison was now ahead by three points. The Hanover guards quickly brought the ball down court. But then Byran slipped, leaving a man free. The free man got the ball and went in for a lay-up. It was good.

With only seconds to go Byran and Willie brought the ball down court. All they had to do was to hold on to the ball and Madison would win. But then, with only four seconds left, one of Byran's passes got away from Dean. The Hanover team got the ball and quickly came down court. A guard fired the ball to their center who flipped it back to him as he cut by. It was a perfect give-and-go. The guard went high into the air for his lay-up. The ball rested on the rim. But as the final bell rang it fell off to one side.

Madison had won by the skin of its teeth. The ball had been on the rim when the bell had gone off. If the ball had dropped in Madison would have lost by one point. They would also have lost a chance at the Championship.

Two days later the school paper came out. The headline read: *Madison Beats Hanover!* The sports writer had written a story about the game with Hanover. She also wrote about the next game that they would play. That was the big one against Morristown for the Championship.

There was a list of all the records of the players on both teams. Joe Kelly's name was listed among the players. Each player was carefully rated. The sports writer thought that the Madison team was a little better. But, she added, only if Joe Kelly plays.

Jamie showed the newspaper to his father.

"Why are you showing me the newspaper, Jamie?" he asked.

Jamie shrugged. He didn't want his father to be disappointed in him. But he didn't want the team to lose because of him either. They had just managed to beat Hanover without Kelly. He didn't think they could beat Morristown. He told this to his father.

"I like to play and I want to win," he said. "But I

know I can't play as well as Joe Kelly. If I don't quit and the team loses, I'll feel awful."

"We always feel bad when we lose, Jamie," his father said. "You know you really can't win or lose for the entire team. Suppose Joe Kelly plays and the team still loses. Won't you feel just as bad?"

"I guess so," Jamie said.

"Well, the final decision is up to you. You should do what you really want to do."

Jamie felt miserable. He wanted to play against Morristown and stay with the team. But he thought he might be blamed if Madison lost. It was all right for his father to be brave. His father didn't have to go to school. And he didn't have to see his name in the school paper.

CHAPTER 8

That night at dinner Jamie decided to have another talk with his father. He was going to tell him that he was going to quit the team. He waited until after they had finished dinner and his father was drinking coffee.

"I'm going to quit the team," he said. There was a small lump in his throat.

"Why?" his father asked.

"Because they need room for a better player," he said.

"I thought you wanted to play."

"It doesn't really matter," Jamie said. "As long as the team wins."

"Oh, I see."

"Anyway, they would rather have Kelly than me on the team."

"I really can't blame them, Jamie." His father pushed away from the table. "You give up so easily. And how do you know they don't want you? Did the coach say something to you?"

"No, but..." Jamie pulled out the crumpled note and showed it to his father. Mr. Davis read it carefully and then gave it back to Jamie.

"Jamie, before you quit the team, will you do me a favor?"

"Yes, if I can," Jamie shrugged.

"Get yourself beaten. Make someone beat you for a spot on the team. That note is telling you to give up without trying. If you believe that you should be on the team, then try. Make someone try harder than you to be on the team. Then if you want to, quit. But don't quit first."

"I guess...I guess so," Jamie replied.

Jamie's father gave him a little push. It was what he did when he was proud of him. But Jamie knew that Kelly was a better ball player. He just knew it.

The next day at practice he didn't talk to anyone. He stayed by himself until Mr. Reese started practice. Mr. Reese said that Joe Kelly would still practice with the team. He said Kelly could help out with the practice. The coach let Joe Kelly play on offense.

The team practiced set plays for fifteen minutes. Jamie was playing defense and he played against Joe. The first play was for Joe to go one-on-one against Jamie. Jamie watched Joe as he moved toward him. He dribbled, stopped, faked, and went up with a high jump shot. Jamie noticed that Joe kept the ball below his waist when he faked a shot. He watched the ball. He watched Joe make a head fake, then go up with the shot. Jamie jumped as high as he could. His fingertips barely touched the ball. But it was enough to knock the shot to the side.

The next play was also aimed at Jamie. This time Joe faked and went easily around Jamie. Another man picked him up but Joe passed off for an easy lay-up. Jamie's man hadn't made the basket but he knew that it was his fault.

The practice went on for another half hour. Most of the plays kept coming at Jamie. And Joe was still making a lot of his shots. Jamie was very tired at the end of practice. He felt that he would never be as good as Kelly. No matter how hard he tried.

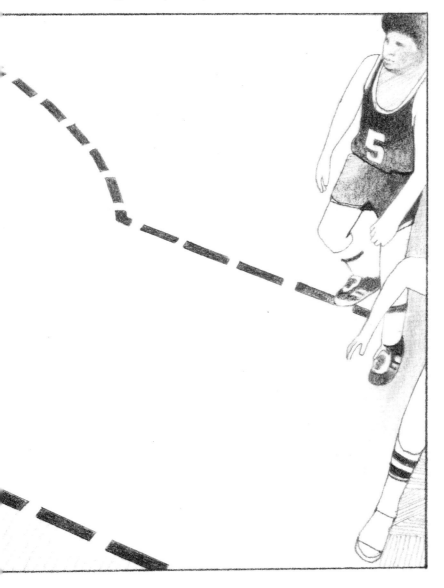

The next day the coach had arranged a special practice game. It was against Newark. And Madison had lost badly. Jamie had played nearly seven minutes and hadn't made any mistakes. He hadn't made any points, either.

After the game Mr. Reese took several of the boys home. Jamie was the last one he dropped off.

"You played a good game tonight, Jamie," Mr. Reese said.

"We lost," Jamie said.

"Newark has a good team. And we did try hard. There's no shame in losing if you do your best."

"If Joe Kelly had been playing, we would have won," Jamie said.

"Maybe yes, and then again, maybe no," said Mr. Reese. "It's easy to say what might have happened. I'll see you at practice tomorrow."

The next day at practice Mr. Reese called a special drill. He said that they had lost to Newark because Newark played better one-on-one than Madison.

"What we're going to practice today is helping each other on defense. We'll play two-man games to begin with. Kelly and Mark are on one team."

Jamie knew that Mr. Reese was going to put him against Kelly. He always put him against Kelly. It seemed like he was trying to show him that Kelly was better. That he, Jamie, should quit the team.

CHAPTER 9

The next day Jamie went to Mr. Reese's office to wait for him. He had been there only a few minutes when Peter walked by. He saw Jamie and went into the office.

"Hi, Jamie," Peter said. "Ready for the big game?"

Jamie shrugged.

"What do you mean by that?" Peter asked.

"I think I'm going to quit the team," Jamie said.

"Oh." Peter sat on the edge of the desk. He looked down at the floor.

"I want to play. Really I do," Jamie said. "But I don't think we can win if I play. With Joe Kelly we have a better chance."

Peter stood up and took a deep breath. "I'm really sorry, Jamie. Because I really want to see you play. I can't play well enough to be out there. But at least you could be out there trying. And I know one thing. You can try just as hard as Joe Kelly or anybody else."

Peter left Mr. Reese's office.

Jamie sat in Mr. Reese's chair. He still didn't know what he should do. He wanted to play, but he didn't want the team to lose. His father had said that he should do what he really wanted to do. But right then he didn't know what that was. Peter had said that he could try just as hard as Kelly. That might be true. But he couldn't shoot as well. He knew that for sure. Just then Mr. Reese came into the office.

"Hello, Jamie. Something bothering you?" he asked as he came into the room.

"I was thinking about the game against Morristown. I was wondering if I should quit the team. Then Joe Kelly could play."

"Oh, I see. Well, in the first place, Jamie, who made you the new coach?"

"No one, Sir."

"Then what makes you so sure that if you quit Kelly will play in your place?"

"I just thought he would."

"I guess you think your quitting will be best for the team?"

"Well, I thought so."

"That's two decisions you have made. One, that if you don't play Joe Kelly will. Two, that your quitting will be best for the team. Anymore you haven't told me about?"

"No, Sir."

"Well, what are you going to do, Jamie? Are you going to decide what the team should do? Or are you going to leave it up to the coach?"

"I'll leave it up to the coach, Sir."

"Okay then. Get me the notes on Morristown. Study and remember them for the game."

Jamie felt a lot better. Perhaps he had been wrong in making decisions by himself. He went over the notes from the Morristown game carefully. He went down the list. He had all the Morristown players listed by number. Number 3 had a good hook shot. Number 11 could shoot from anywhere. Number 12 always dribbled the ball twice before he shot. Each player's habits were written down. He didn't know what the coach had

in mind, but he would do the best he could.

On the way home he dropped by Peter's house. He told him that he was going to play. Peter was happy and he wished him luck.

When Jamie got home he told his father that he was going to play. His father said that he would take the day off from work. It would be the first time that he would see him play. And it would be for the Championship.

CHAPTER 10

On the day of the big game the stands were filled. They were playing at Morristown. Jamie looked around to see if he could see his parents. He finally saw them sitting behind the scorer's table. He hoped he would not disappoint them.

Most of Morristown's players were bigger than Madison's. Jamie could not help watching them warm up. Some of their players could stuff the ball into the basket. After what seemed a long time the buzzer rang. When both teams sat down, the names of all the players were called out. When his name was called, Jamie ran out to stand with his teammates. He could see the students from Madison applauding. He could also feel the excitement in the air.

When the game started the ball went up and down the court quickly as each team scored. First Madison was ahead, then Morristown. Then slowly Morristown began to creep ahead. They had a four-point lead. Then it went to six. Madison was playing as never before. But Morristown just kept scoring and scoring. Jamie sat and watched his teammates fall behind. At the half, Madison was behind by eight points.

In the locker room the team was exhausted. They had played as well as they could. But still they were losing.

"All right, guys," Mr. Reese said. "What's happening is that they're simply outscoring us. The score is 36 to 28. That's a very high score. We can score against them. What we have to do is stop them from scoring so much. Especially their number 12. He's got nearly half their points. When Jamie and Mark went to see them play before, he

also scored the most points. So what we have to do is stop him from scoring. I'll put a good defensive man on him. If we can stop him, the rest of their team will be forced to shoot. Does everyone understand?"

Everyone nodded.

"Jamie is going to guard their number 12. Don't worry about scoring, Jamie. Just keep your man from scoring. If you can stop Joe Kelly in practice, you should be able to stop him. Now, let's go."

The two teams warmed up again. Jamie now knew why Mr. Reese always had him playing against Kelly in practice. His hands were sweating and his mouth was dry. Finally the referee blew his whistle. The second half was about to begin.

The first time that number 12 got the ball Jamie fouled him. He made the foul shot easily. A moment later Mark scored on a long jump shot from the corner.

Morristown brought the ball down. Number 12 got the ball in the corner. He dribbled once and faked with his head. Then he tried to go around Jamie. Jamie guarded him closely and he passed the ball away. A moment later he had the ball again. He faked left and took two quick dribbles to the right. Jamie knew that he would shoot. When he went up for the shot, Jamie went up with him. At the top of his jump, number 12 let the ball go. But Jamie's hands were right there and he blocked the shot. Byran got the ball and went down for the lay-up. It was good.

Morristown got the ball and scored on a tap-in. Dean scored on a short hook and Morristown tried a fast break. Number 12 was trailing the lead man. Jamie went down court as fast as he could. He was watching for the pass-off on the break. Dean and Mark went over to stop the ball. But the front man flipped the ball back to number 12. He stopped and went up for the jumper. Jamie went up but missed the ball. The shot hit the rim and bounced away. Byran picked off the rebound and soon Madison scored again. Morristown called time out.

"Now we'll see how they adjust to us," Mr. Reese said. He smiled at Jamie.

When the ball went back into play the Morristown players spread out. None of them were near the basket. Then they passed the ball to number 12. Jamie realized what they were up to. They had spread out so that his man could go one-on-one with him. Number 12 came driving in. Jamie was ready for him. He faked left, then tried to pass Jamie on the right. Jamie didn't go for the fake. And number 12 went right into him. It was an offensive foul. The ball went to Madison.

Madison scored again. And Morristown called another time out. Mr. Reese was very excited. He told them to keep up the good play. Jamie looked at the scoreboard. Madison was ahead, 46 to 43.

When time was back in, number 12 stayed on the outside. The rest of his team played close to the middle. Neither team scored for the next minute. But then Morristown hit from the outside. Madison answered with a lay-up by Mark.

The buzzer rang just as Morristown was about to make the inbounds pass. The players looked up. The game was over! They had won!

The next thing Jamie knew they were all running for the locker room. Everyone was shouting and slapping each other on the back. Madison had won!

The next day the school paper carried the story. Mr. Reese brought Jamie a copy. There was a picture of Dean holding the trophy they had won. The caption read:

MADISON UPSETS MORRISTOWN
AS CAPTAIN SCORES 16 POINTS.

There was one line circled. It read that Jamie Davis was the only Madison player who did not score. But it also said that his defensive playing had given Madison a winning edge. Next to it in big letters was written: *THANKS FROM THE TEAM.*